Gliding with Glisten, The Fairhope Dragon

Story by Debby Hackbarth
Illustrations by Carter Hlavin, Debby Hackbarth, and Jonah Hackbarth

ISBN: 978-1-95693-64-7

FV-7

Published by:
Intellect Publishing, LLC
www.IntellectPublishing.com

Visit the website:
www.TheFairhopeDragonBook.com

Dedication:

To my husband, Jim, for his unconditional love and daily encouragement.

To my grandchildren, Katarina, Jonah, Carter, and Kaleb for their love and strength of character – the inspiration for this story.

Thanks:

To Carter, Jonah, and Savannah
for their extremely talented
artwork.

To Jim, Rebekah, Carter, and
Toni for their fantastic editing
assistance.

Gliding with Glisten, The Fairhope Dragon

It is said that dragons and other winged creatures have existed in various times throughout the Earth.

Glisten's story is more than a fairy tale; it is a tale of two young people who exhibited bravery and compassion.

Katarina and her twin brother Kaleb lived on a small patch of land on the bank of Fish River just east of the lovely hamlet of Fairhope, Alabama.

Long ago, the village of Fairhope was known as Alabama City.

The abundant seafood in the Fish River included freshwater species (red drum and spotted seatrout) in the upper part of the river and saltwater fish (flounder and speckled trout) in the lower part of the river, close to Weeks Bay. Weeks Bay connected the Fish River to a part of Mobile Bay which emptied into the Gulf of Mexico.

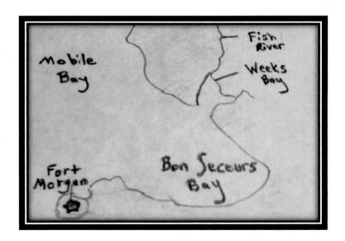

Sporadically, grass shrimp were found in the river - a special treat for dragons.

These tiny shrimps lived among the marshland grasses and were light pink in color - almost transparent. The grass shrimp were known by another name - popcorn shrimp.

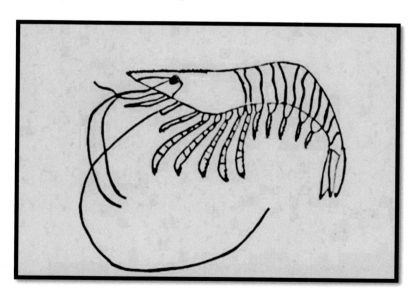

The dragons were able to find the popcorn shrimp because of the bulging eyes that protruded from the heads of the shrimp.

The twins were orphaned because their parents had died from snake bites while collecting berries to make jam. It was very difficult for the twins because they were only seven years old at that time. A retired teacher named Mariposa or Butterfly knew their parents, so she watched over the twins.

She taught them to read, write, and do mathematics. The twins loved Mariposa like a grandmother.

Katarina and Kaleb were ten years old when Glisten came into their lives.

Mariposa took care of several animals on her property. The warm climate of Southern Alabama and the abundant vegetation helped the cows, chickens, and goats to thrive. Mariposa gave Katarina and Kaleb several animals to care for so the twins could learn to be independent.

One day Kaleb was examining his troubled cow named Bovine, when he heard a strange sound from under a pile of straw nearby. Kaleb knew that Katarina liked to take in stray animals and he thought that this noise might be coming from one of those creatures.

Kaleb called for Katarina so that she could identify the strange noise, but she did not answer. He quickly decided to hide behind a large bag in the small barn so that he could remain safe.

Kaleb was about to come out from behind the bag when Katarina danced into the small barn. She was singing a song that Mariposa had taught them and she did not notice Kaleb.

Katarina's splendid singing startled the young dragon, who was hiding in the straw. Even though the dragon was only six feet long, she was able to fly. The dragon flew right over Kaleb's head and almost crashed into Katarina!

The animal's skin and scales were so dazzling that neither child was alarmed by the sudden flight. The twins were fascinated at her body which brightly shone in green, teal, and cobalt blue. They named her Glisten because her body glistened in the sunlight.

The twins were not sure what type of animal she was, but they thought the creature might be in the reptilian family because her slim body was covered with scales. Her head looked like the head of a serpent; however, her wings were huge and graceful like a large bat.

Katarina and Kaleb agreed that they would seek Mariposa's advice after they made sure that Bovine and the airborne animal were safe. Before they left the small barn, they filled a bucket with milk for Glisten.

Mariposa told the twins that they had probably encountered a dragon. The village residents had not seen one of these stunning bay-dwelling creatures for decades.

Mariposa wanted to help the children raise Glisten.

When the trio arrived back at the small barn, they found Glisten's bucket of milk next to Bovine, who was licking Glisten as she slept. Mariposa marveled at Glisten's beauty during her peaceful sleep. It seemed like Bovine was grooming or cleaning Glisten as though the dragon was her calf.

The twins needed to build a structure to house the young dragon. Since Mariposa had studied dragons, she knew that Glisten might grow to one hundred feet long with a wing span of fifty feet. Fortunately, a large old barn in need of repair, stood at the rear of Mariposa's property close to the intersection of the Fish River and Weeks Bay.

Kaleb ran to get the tractor with its trailer so he could head out and inspect the old barn. The girls stayed in the small barn and got to know Glisten. When Kaleb returned, he commented that the old barn was stable and that it would work for now.

Glisten was a bit hesitant around the trio. It may have been because she had never been in close proximity to humans. Mariposa guessed that like other animals in the area, Glisten had been surviving on fish, snakes, and rodents. Glisten hesitated to taste the milk until Katarina successfully encouraged Glisten to drink the milk from the bucket.

Kaleb went inside the small barn with the girls so that he could become acquainted with Glisten. As the humans continued to speak softly to Glisten, a new friendship was born.

As Glisten grew, the twins needed to enlarge and improve the old barn. They could buy the necessary materials because Mariposa was an entrepreneur. Mariposa sold her books, chicken eggs, goat and cow milk, and leather goods at a roadside stand.

Day-after-day, the twins enjoyed romping with Glisten throughout the property after they finished their daily lessons. On fishing trips, they loved watching Glisten ascend and then dive into the bay and along the shore. Glisten was hunting for seafood — especially the popcorn shrimp.

When the air was cooler during twilight, Glisten would love to soar from the land, along the river, and then over the bay. The children would have loved to watch her for hours; however, they still had chores to do around the farm.

After chores were finished on the weekends, Mariposa watched the twins riding Glisten. Mariposa rode Glisten as well, but not as often. The workday week could not conclude fast enough so the fantastic flying could begin. As long as the dragon wished to fly, the trio enjoyed gliding with Glisten in southeastern Alabama and northwestern Florida.

Fairhope and the surrounding towns grew significantly over the years. As the population continued to increase, the timing of their flights became increasingly more important. The trio did not want Glisten to be seen for her safety and well-being.

Kaleb learned to work with leather and he created saddles for all three of them. He needed to make sure that the saddles were as comfortable as possible for the humans as well as for Glisten. As the years progressed, Kaleb fashioned new saddles to accommodate their changing bodies.

Mariposa taught Katarina how to work beautiful floral designs into leather. Later, Katarina would use this knowledge to create lovely leather coats and vests to sell at their roadside stand and at local markets.

Throughout the remainder of their childhood, the twins worked alongside Mariposa as she taught Glisten how to protect Bovine, guard the farm, and take the three of them for flights around the countryside.

Living with a dragon that grew from six feet to eventually ninety feet was quite the daunting task. The twins lovingly cared for Glisten by enlarging her barn often, providing about ten gallons of milk daily, and making sure that she felt cherished and safe.

They respected Glisten's need to fly as many as three hours per day. Kaleb and Katarina continued to follow Mariposa's gifted guidance as she assisted them in their interactions with Glisten. Mariposa's leadership prepared the twins for life; whether they lived on the farm or in a village – like nearby Fairhope.

When the twins reached the age of fifteen, they observed Mariposa riding Glisten less often. Mariposa was sixty years old when she came into their lives. Because her life had been difficult physically, her body was becoming more fragile with each passing year.

One warm spring day, Mariposa ascended onto Glisten's back and they flew northeast toward the forestlands which are currently known as the Weeks Bay National Estuarine Research Reserve.

The twins thought they would never see the Mariposa or the beautiful dragon again and they longed to take a journey to find Mariposa and Glisten. Also, they wanted to see if Glisten had ever been reunited with her mother. The memories of their adventure-filled childhood journey with the fantastic dragon would remain with them for a very long time.

Made in the USA
Middletown, DE
05 December 2022